WONGUTHA TALES

WONGUTHA TALES

BAWOO STORIES & BADUDU STORIES

MAY L. O'BRIEN

 FREMANTLE PRESS

CONTENTS

BAWOO STORIES

These stories are dedicated to the Wongutha elders. They helped us to realise that having rules and keeping them is vital for group survival and living together.

In the language of the Wongutha people, Bawoo means a long time ago. These are stories which were handed down from generation to generation of the Wongutha people. They are unique to Wongutha Country. Other groups who lived in different places have their own language and own stories to tell about how things began. These stories came from a time when there was little contact between different groups.

Stories such as these were told so that children would come to understand their land, their people and their beginnings. The stories had a particular purpose and were an important part of the children's education.

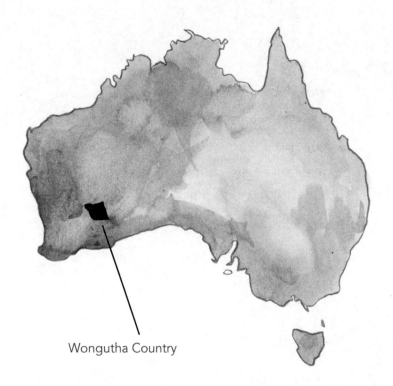

Wongutha Country

How crows became black explains how the crows who were grey wanted to change colour because no one liked their silver-grey feathers. They felt left out and thought if they were black they would be accepted.

HOW CROWS BECAME BLACK

Long long ago, on a hot and stormy night, a flock of crows flew into the Eastern Goldfields of Western Australia. It seemed as if they had been blown in by the storm. No one had seen them in these parts before. They were not like the crows of today. Those crows of long ago were silver-grey and they travelled in large flocks. However, like the crows we see today, the silver-grey crows perched in the tall trees where they built their nests on the highest branches. From these high perches, their sharp eyes could see everything below.

Each morning, when the sun rose in the east, the crows soared lazily, high high in the sky. They flapped their wings occasionally, while they waited for strong gusts of wind. These gusts took them gliding over the hills and plains below. As they flew, the sun touched their feathers making them sparkle and glitter. From below, the crows looked like twinkling stars or something from outer space, moving in and out of the low and wispy clouds.

The crows loved the bushland and soon knew every tree, hill, creek and valley. They loved the freedom to fly over all they could see. Only one thing about their new home spoilt their happiness.

The other birds didn't like the silver-grey crows at all. They were jealous of the way the crows' feathers glistened and sparkled in the bright sunlight. They never missed an opportunity to make nasty remarks about the crows as they passed them in the bush.

'Look at old shiny feathers,' they would jeer as the crows flew by. This teasing upset the crows.

The animals didn't like the crows either. They were frightened by the glinting of the crows' dazzling feathers. The kangaroos and wallabies moved to the plains and far-off hills, where they would eat without being disturbed. The lizards scurried to the trees. They buried themselves under leaves and dead branches and waited until it was safe to come out. The snakes too became restless. They grew tired of staying in stuffy holes and logs whenever the crows were near.

The crows annoyed the Wongutha people as well. Every day the men hunted for food and every day they came home empty-handed. They searched over the plains and in the nearby hills, but the animals had gone. The people became hungrier and hungrier and the men became angrier and angrier.

'Ngaliba gugagu manu, bardu garngalu ngurluthunu' (When we go hunting, those crows flash by and frighten everything), they growled. 'Marlu birni ngabathi mungarra mabithangu' (We will never get meat for our families).

No one wanted the crows near them. Each time they flew by, the people raised their fists in the air.

'Wandigadi ngalibanha' (Keep away from us).

'Nhurra yunthugarranu, thanalgudu mabitha' (Go somewhere, where you will not annoy anyone), they yelled at the top of their voices.

The crows were upset by the people's anger and talked about it.

'Gark! Gark! Why is everyone angry with us?' they squawked.

'All the bush creatures are angry with us,' said a wise old crow. 'The lizards and insects hide under leaves and dead branches and the snakes stay hidden in their holes when we're near. The cheeky birds chase us whenever we pass by. We haven't any friends at all.' The other crows looked at each other and nodded.

'What can we do to make everyone happy again? Why don't other creatures like us?' croaked the old crow as big tears began to trickle down his silver-grey face.

The crows, seeing the tears on the old one's face, all started to cry and the trees shook with the noise of their loneliness.

'Gar-ark, gar-ark,' they cried. 'Gar-ark, gar-ark.' The wailing of the unhappy crows floated through the bush and gullies. The other birds and animals were surprised and wondered what was wrong.

Day after day, day after day, the crows went on and on. Their tears flowed down their faces and onto the ground. There, the tears formed creeks and made salt lakes on the plains. The animals wondered if the crows would ever stop.

After a long time, when the crows could cry no more, they turned to the old crow for advice.

'What can we do? How can we change, so that we can make friends?' they asked. The old crow thought for a while.

'It's our silver-grey colour that gets us into trouble. We must change to blend in with the bushland,' he said. The young crows thought this was a good idea.

'The Wongutha people have dark skin. We should be like them,' said one.

'But how can we become black?' asked another.

'Sometimes, the Wongutha men paint white ochre on their bodies. We can do the same with black ochre,' replied the old crow.

The next day the crows flew off to look for black ochre. They searched in dry creek beds and looked in caves. They flew over plains and over the salt lakes. But they couldn't find any black ochre. The crows flew to some red sandhills and started to scratch in the sand, but all they found was fine red sand. Some of the crows searched among the trees. All they found here was some sticky gum. They found no black ochre.

The tired crows sat in the trees and watched the women below. They were cooking their meat on the open fires. The meat was red when they put it into the flames and black when they took it out.

'That's what we must do!' exclaimed one of the crows. 'We must go into the cooking fires to become black.'

'No, we don't have to do that,' said the wise old crow. 'We can wait until the men burn the bush. Then the flames make a wide path.'

A few weeks later the Wongutha men started to burn off the bush. They did this to make it fresh and green again. The old crow saw the men start the fires and called the others together. He told them what to do.

'Stand still,' he said. 'Wait for the fire. Don't move until I say.'

The crows trembled as they waited for the fire to come. Their sharp, beady eyes darted here and there as they watched. Nervously, they ruffled their feathers as they stood still.

They didn't have long to wait. The crackling fire raced towards them. It burned through spinifex, dry grass and dead leaves in its path. Every now and then, flames shot high over bushes and small trees. The fire roared and crackled and spat out red, fiery cinders. Closer and closer came the leaping flames.

Soon the fire swept over and around the trembling crows as they stood in its path. How brave they were! Then, everything was silent and still.

The old crow stirred, opened his eyes and looked around.

'It's all over!' he shouted. 'It's all over!'

Slowly at first, the other crows opened their

eyes too. They looked around. The bush looked bare and black. They shivered as they turned and looked at each other. How horrible they looked in only their wrinkly skin. Their beautiful silver-grey feathers were gone.

The young crows silently gathered around the old crow and waited for him to speak again.

'You have been very brave,' he said. 'Our feathers will soon grow again. Then we will be proud of ourselves.'

For what seemed a long time, the crows hid themselves while their feathers grew. They were worried. Would the new feathers still be silver-grey?

At last they came out of their hiding places. How handsome they looked. Their new feathers were shiny black. Proudly, the crows strutted about. Their white eyes gleamed happily as everyone looked at them.

'Are they new birds?' asked the animals.

'No! They are the crows,' replied the birds sharply.

'They are beautiful new feathers,' exclaimed

the animals. The old crow turned, smiled and winked at the others.

'Now, the animals and birds can move about in the bush without running away from us,' he said proudly. 'Our new feathers make us more like them. We must also try to live apart and never to fly in big flocks.'

Today, we can still see the salt lakes made by the tears of the silver-grey crows of long ago, and also the salt bushes that soaked up their salty tears. The black crows are now an important part of our Australian bush. They are not the same as those silver-grey ones of long ago. Crows no longer travel in large flocks and they keep apart from everyone. They never make good friends with other bush creatures and small birds still chase them away.

Why the emu can't fly describes how vanity leads to loss of power and position.

WHY THE EMU CAN'T FLY

At the beginning of time, Wongutha stories tell us, emus could fly. They were the biggest birds in the air and there were many of them. When they flew in their great flocks, they looked like dark clouds moving lazily across the sky.

The emus could see many things happening. They saw the smoke from the people's camp fires as it floated upwards. They watched and laughed as a playful gubi-gubi (whirlwind) thrashed through the bush. Twisting and twirling, it gathered up the sticks and leaves in its path, then tossed them back to the ground.

The emus liked everything they saw and felt pleased with themselves.

Everyone in the bush seemed happy enough.

The small birds shared the space in the sky and the animals moved peacefully through the bush.

Because the emus were big and powerful, they felt better than the other birds. Then, things began to change. The emus tossed their heads into the air and became quite snooty. They began to think they were the greatest and fastest birds that ever flew. No-one could be better than them, they thought! It wasn't bad to think that they were the best, but the emus started to boast about it.

'We can fly higher and faster than anyone else,' they bragged. They looked around to make sure that everyone was looking and listening.

Day after day, week after week and month after month the emus went on with their silly antics. They became even more boastful and the other birds grew tired of them.

The emus became nastier and meaner.

'Let's play a trick on the small birds next time they come flying with us,' they said.

The next morning, the emus were waiting for the other birds. They flew around them, flapping their huge, dusty wings. If that didn't scare the little ones, their next trick did. With wings held high and their heads bent low, their eyes mean and savage, the emus rushed at the small birds. The little birds struggled to stop themselves from crashing into the big, fat emu bullies, who laughed out loud. This bullying went on for a long time, and soon the small birds lost the will to sing. The land became quiet. The people and the animals missed the singing of the birds and wondered why the bush was so silent.

The small birds grew angry with themselves and cried.

'Why do we let the emus do this to us? There must be something we can do to stop them from bullying us.' They were sad and miserable and they sat in the trees and sulked. The people saw what was happening and they felt sorry for the little birds.

'Garlaya birnigu wiyardu ngurlurri' (Don't be afraid of the emus). 'Binangga gulila. Thana yalbrinhba nhurrabanha wandigadigu' (Think of some way that you can stop them).

'We don't know what to do,' replied the birds, 'but one thing is for sure, we've had enough! We're not going to take any more of those stupid tricks from those big, fat, bullying birds.'

But, what could small birds do? The emus were too powerful for any little birds.

At last, the birds thought of something that might help them stop the emus bullying. Quickly, they flew off to see the wedge-tailed eagles. The birds found them in a bush clearing, where they were feeding.

'We need your help,' said the small birds nervously. 'We want you to chase the emus out of the sky.' Always ready for a fight, the wedge-tailed eagles agreed to help them.

'We'll ask the hawks to join us,' they said between mouthfuls, while they pulled and tore at their meal.

The eagles and hawks joined forces to try to chase the emus from the sky. However, even this powerful team couldn't defeat the emus. The emus were too big and strong.

When the small birds appeared the next day,

the emus mocked and jeered.

'Hah! Hah! Hah! Your measly old plan didn't work, did it? No one can chase us out of the sky. Not even the hawks and eagles can do that! We're too smart for them and we're too smart for you!'

In desperation, the unhappy birds turned to the animals for help. The animals sat thinking before they answered.

'We have watched the way the emus behave and we know how well they can fly. We have seen them showing off and we are upset too. But we have to live in the bush with the emus and we don't want to upset them. We're sorry. There's nothing we can do to help you.'

The small birds flew off, angry and upset that the animals had refused to help.

'Our last chance is to ask the pink and grey galahs. They seem to have an answer for every-thing,' they said to each other. Immediately, they flew off to see them.

The galahs listened to the other birds' story. Then, after a lot of talking amongst themselves, they suggested what they thought was a good idea.

'Really, there's only one thing that you can do,' said the galahs. 'You must wait for the nesting time of the emus. When the eggs have been laid, rush in and crack all of them. Then you won't ever have to worry about the emus again.'

'What a terrible suggestion! We can't do that! We wouldn't like anyone doing that to *our* eggs!' whispered the little birds to each other. 'But, we are desperate, and we *must* do something soon. We *will* do as the galahs have suggested.'

The small birds didn't have long to wait for the egg-laying season to begin. When it was time, each of the female emus laid between six and nine big, beautiful, dark green eggs. Then they flew off. It was the male emus' job to sit on the eggs.

'Did you see that? The females have all gone off and left their eggs to the males,' said the surprised little birds.

Every day the small birds sat quietly and patiently in the trees and watched. They were waiting for the emus to take a rest from sitting on the eggs. Finally, the break came. The emus stood up and stretched and moved away.

'Here's our chance,' said the anxious little birds. 'Quickly, get to the eggs and crack them all.' With one swoop, the small birds flew down and stood by the large eggs. The emus saw them and charged back. Terrified, the small birds flew off.

Once again the small birds went to the galahs.

'We tried to do as you said, but we were too afraid of the angry emus,' moaned the little birds.

Feeling ashamed, they turned their heads away and begged, 'Please galahs, do help us again.'

'We've run out of ideas,' replied the galahs in a 'we-can't-be-bothered' tone. 'Go to the older Wongutha men. Those elders will tell you what to do.'

When it was nearly day, the small birds went to the elders. 'Would you please help us get rid of the emus?' asked the small birds. 'They won't share the sky with us anymore.' There was a long pause before the elders answered.

'Garlaya wiyardu mirrindalgu' (We won't kill the emus). 'Gugagu guthugu mirrindalgu' (We only kill what we need to eat). 'Bundu yirna yudinthu nhurrabanha wathalgu' (But our head man will tell you what to do). 'Balu ngurra guthubangga nyinarranhi' (He is away now). 'Balu githili gutharrangga ngalalgu' (He'll be back in a few months time). 'Nhurra balugudu wangga' (You must talk to him).

The birds were pleased with the advice that the elders gave and decided to wait in the trees not far away.

A few months later, a messenger came and said that the head man would meet the small birds under the mulga tree. The elder arrived on time. He looked at each one of the little birds. They sensed that he was a very important man and they became quiet.

Speaking in a loud, clear voice, the elder said, 'Ngayulu nhurrabagu balalgu' (I'll help you). 'Ngayulu garlayagudu durlgu yingagu' (I'll sing a special song for the emus). 'Nhurraba nyina guyula wardangga' (You must wait in the trees).

'Nhurraba balul nyina nhagugu' (Then you will see what happens).

The man looked straight ahead and started to sing in a high-pitched voice. It was an old song from the past, a song handed down by their ancestors to special Wongutha men. The emus heard the singing and flew in from every direction. They gathered around the man and listened.

When the words of the song had faded away, the man turned and disappeared into the bush. For a while the emus just stood there, not knowing what to do or where to turn.

That night, the bush was quiet. Not a sound could be heard. Not even the cicadas or night owls made a noise. While everyone was asleep, something very strange happened to the emus as they ran through the bush in the moonlight. It was very, very strange.

At daybreak, when the emus thought no-one was watching, they ran to a clearing in the bush. There, they stretched and flapped their wings to fly away. But nothing happened. Their wings had become stumpy and too small to fly. The emus ran about in panic. They spread their wings and tried to lift off in the breeze. Nothing happened. They tried again and again and again. They stood on a black stump and jumped, thinking that that might help, but still nothing happened. It was useless. The emus were baffled. They questioned each other. Then, they remembered the words of the song, they had heard the day before.

'Garlaya darldu birni, ngayunha gulila' (You boastful emus, listen to me).

'Nhurraba ngula barrbagu, nhurra ngula barrbagu' (You won't ever fly again, you won't ever fly again).

'Ngaba nhurraba dirdu, jinangga barnangga barrabithagu' (From now on, you will only walk and run).

Suddenly, the emus understood the meaning of that special song the important man had sung.

The small birds sitting in the trees had been watching as the emus jumped up and down and flapped about. It was a funny sight. Now, it was the small birds' turn to laugh. They laughed so much that they nearly fell off the branches. They began singing and feeling cheerful again.

'Isn't this wonderful? We have the sky to ourselves,' they chirped merrily as they flew up into the open sky. They had room to spread their wings, to swoop, to dive, to glide again. The sky now looked a bigger and brighter place and the air certainly smelt fresh and sweet. The bush was filled with bird songs again, and the birds felt good. It was time for a celebration.

The small birds hurried to thank the Wongutha elders. They told them what had happened. The Wonguthas felt sorry for the emus, but they were pleased that the birds were feeling much happier.

'Garlaya garnbirringu. Thana barrabithanhi ngalibal dawarra' (One good thing about all of this is that now the emus can wander through the bush with us). 'Gabi nhanganha burlganha garlayagu, nhurra ngalibagu' (This country is big enough for us all). 'Garlaya birni garnanh-garnanh wiyarringu' (The emus have learned not to boast). 'Thana yungarra barrabithagu' (Now they mind their own business).

The kangaroos who wanted to be people tells what happens when walking kangaroos disobey the rules. It helps to explain why some places or areas are out of bounds to children.

THE KANGAROOS WHO WANTED TO BE PEOPLE

A long, long time ago, when the world began, kangaroos walked in the same way as people. They wanted to learn how to become people and they often hid near the Wongutha people's camp and watched them. The Wongutha men watched the kangaroos too, and they talked as they made their boomerangs, shields and strong sharp spears.

'Marlu thana yarlbrinhba' (Those kangaroos are strange), they said. 'Ngaliba nharrabrinh wiyardu nhangungu. Thana ngaliba brinhba' (We never see other animals that walk like us). 'Guthubanggu ngalibanha wiyardu nhaguranhi'

(Other animals don't watch us like those kangaroos do). The kangaroos and the people watched each other while pretending not to.

One day, the kangaroos saw a man searching among the trees. They crept up behind him and watched secretly. They saw the man sit down and rub two sticks together. As the sticks became hot, the man added some dry grass. The grass smoked, then caught alight and soon there was a crackling, hissing fire. The kangaroos looked at each other in surprise.

'We must learn how to make a fire too,' they said. 'We must learn all these people secrets.'

In the evenings, the people gathered around their fires and talked and sang. They told stories about the long, long ago, while the children listened. Sometimes, the stories made the children laugh, but at other times, the stories made them think or made them a little afraid.

In the evenings, the kangaroos in the shadows crept closer to listen and to try and learn the secrets of the people.

Although the kangaroos overheard the stories

and songs, important secrets were kept by the elders. These were never talked about in front of women and children, and the elders certainly would never tell the kangaroos or any other animals. So, the kangaroos didn't learn anything important by creeping about in the shadows and listening.

One day, the Wongutha men decided to take a long walk into the bush. It was time to visit a very special place. The kangaroos saw them off and followed them. The men walked over many hills until at last they entered a large cave.

The cave was deep and on its walls were interesting paintings. These had been painted a long time ago. They were important to the Wongutha people, because they were painted by the people's ancestors. It was a very special place indeed.

In the cave the men prepared for a ceremony. First they crushed red and white ochre and took great care in painting their special symbols on their faces and bodies. Then, it was time for the singing and dancing which re-told the stories of their ancestors.

The men's feet pounded heavily on the ground and made the dust fly. When they came to the end of a dance the men flicked up the dust with their toes and gave a loud shout. Then, another song and dance would begin and the dust would fly again. The cave echoed with the words of these old songs.

The kangaroos watched the men perform their dances. Then they followed them back to the camp and watched from the shadows as often as possible. The kangaroos learned much. Soon, they wanted to be treated as people. They went to the Wongutha people and said, 'We have watched all you do. We want to live with you.' The men said, 'Nhurra ngalibanh brinhba wiya' (You can never be like us). 'Nhurra Wongutha brinhba wiya' (You can never be people).

However, the kangaroos now believed they *were* people and tried to do the same kind of things.

Early one morning, a man spotted the kangaroos as they crept to the cave. Immediately, he told the elders who became angry. They marched out to stop the kangaroos but met them in the bush near the camp.

'Nhurraba ngalibagagu bulbangga tharrbagadingu' (You have been to our cave), they said. 'Ngaliba burdu wathanu nhurrabanha' (We have warned you not to go there), 'nhurraba dirdu mabithanh bulba nhagura' (but you still visit the cave). 'Nhurraba wala mabithagu, ngaliba ngaba nhurrabanha bunggugu' (If it happens again, we will have to punish you).

The kangaroos would not listen. They cheekily flicked their tails at the men and laughed.

The next day, they visited the cave again. They continued to break the rules of the Wongutha people and disobey the elders. The elders became very worried and decided to ask their head man for help.

The head man called the kangaroos to a special meeting, at the camp meeting ground. The women and children were told to stay away because it wasn't their business. The head man, the elders and the kangaroos gathered in a circle.

Everyone waited and was silent.

Before the head man could speak, a big gubi-gubi (whirlwind) blew across the gathering. The children ran from their mothers, who were in the bushes at the other end of the camp, and into the middle of the gubi-gubi. It twirled and spun and the children merrily shouted and squealed. They tried to keep up with it, but it was much too fast and cunning for them.

The men were angry and shouted at the children to stop. They had been warned not to come near. The men got their boomerangs and tapped them together as they hummed and sang the gubi-gubi away. The children saw the anger in the men's faces and stopped their play. They ran back to their mothers in the bushes.

After a while, when everything was quiet again, the head man stood up. He turned to the kangaroos.

'Ngaliba burdu wathanu, ngalibanha wanaranhi wandi' (We have warned you to stop following us) 'nhurraba bina widu-widu birni' (but you ignore us). 'Ngaba nhurrabanha ngaliba bunggugu' (Now you will be punished). 'Nhurra ngalibanha wanaranhi wandi' (You will stop following us). 'Ngabathi nhurraba ngalibanh nhagu ngulurrigu, nhurraba worl-worl mabithagu' (Instead, when you see us, you will be afraid and hop away quickly). 'Ngaliba nhurrabanha gugagu bunggugu. (We will hunt you and you will be meat for us). 'Nhurra Wongutha brinhba wiya rurra marlgu' (You will never again be able to walk like us). 'Nhurra ngabathi worl-worl mabithagu' (From now on, you will hop on your back legs).

The head man stopped talking. He stood quite still and stared at the kangaroos. The kangaroos were afraid because they knew that the head man was very important and had special powers. There was not a sound. Then the head man looked into the distance and began to sing. At first he sang softly. Then his song became louder and louder. At last his voice faded into a whisper.

As the kangaroos stood listening to the haunting music, they slowly began to change. Their back legs and their tails grew longer and longer, while their front legs became smaller and smaller.

With the last note of the song, the head man went behind the bushes and to his camp. For a long time, the kangaroos stood still and silent. They felt dazed and strange.

Finally, they looked around. Where was the head man? Where were the other men? The kangaroos were alone. They stared at each other, trying to understand the changes they saw. Then they turned, and together they hopped away to the tall trees. The bush and trees were to be their home now. Never again would they live near people.

Since that time, kangaroos move in family groups. Instead of walking, they hop on their back legs. Much time is spent lying and sleeping in the shade of trees. They need to be on the lookout for people and always try to keep away from them.

Barn-Barn Barlala, the bush trickster tells of children who take no notice of warnings and wander off into the bush. Survival skills learned from their elders help to save them.

BARN-BARN BARLALA, THE BUSH TRICKSTER

'I wish that the barrga-barrga (wild mistletoe berries) would hurry up and ripen,' said one of the girls. 'I really like them!'

'They'll be ready soon,' a boy replied. 'Gabarli (grandmother) says that they are nearly ripe now.'

The next day, the children noticed that the birds were busy at the trees. The knew what that meant.

'Hurry up,' they shouted to each other. 'The birds are eating our berries. They must be ripe.'

Quickly they all ran into the bush and to their favourite trees.

'I hope the birds haven't eaten all the berries,'

said one.

'No. There are plenty up high where the sun gets them,' called back another.

As the children began to climb the trees, the birds watched and kept still. They didn't like the children eating *their* fruit.

'What will we do?' asked one of the birds. 'Those children are very noisy and they will eat all the berries.' The birds sat silently. They were watching and thinking.

'Who can we ask to help us frighten the children away?' they asked each other.

'I can help you. I know what to do,' said Barn-Barn Barlala.

Barn-Barn Barlala flew off to the barrga-barrga trees. He hid behind the branches and began to call out. The children stopped and listened. They were frightened. They remembered what gabarli had told them.

'Don't follow Barn-Barn Barlala,' she had warned.

'Let's get away from here,' the children said as they climbed out of the trees.

'You're not afraid, are you?' said one boy to his sister. 'It's only a bird and it won't hurt us.' The other children didn't wait. They were off.

Then the brother and sister heard the call again. This time Barn-Barn Barlala seemed to call them from the south. Again Barn-Barn Barlala called, but now it seemed to come from the north. That bird was very clever. He could trick people every time.

The boy and girl forgot gabarli's warning and listened to the beautiful call.

'Let's see if we can find the bird?' the boy coaxed his sister. 'It's not far away.'

As they followed the sweet sound of that tricky bird, they wandered further and further into the bush. Each time they heard the bird's call, it seemed to come from a long way off. They couldn't seem to get any closer to it.

At the end of the day, they were very tired and miserable. They sat down under a big tree and were soon fast asleep.

Early next morning, the children woke and looked around. They didn't know where they were. The bush looked different.

'I don't know this country.' The boy sounded scared. 'I've never been here before.'

'We're lost,' his sister replied, 'and I'm hungry and thirsty. We should never have listened to Barn-Barn Barlala.'

'Don't worry,' the boy was trying to sound brave. 'I can find our way home.'

'How?' asked the little girl. 'This is all new bushland to us.'

'I know,' came the reply, 'but I can find out the way we came. Dad always told me to look behind me as well as where I'm going. While we were following Barn-Barn Barlala, I kept looking back. Dad taught me to look for tracks on the ground too.' When she heard this, his sister felt much happier.

The two children began their long walk home. The boy's eyes moved everywhere. He kept pointing out the trees and rocks that they had passed the day before.

'See this tree with the broken branch, we saw that yesterday.'

Quickly they walked through the bush. This time when they heard Barn-Barn Barlala's call, they did not stop and listen.

At last, they heard voices calling them in the distance. Their family and friends were looking for them. They were very worried.

'Ngaliba nhangagudu' (We're over here), shouted the children when they saw the people through the trees. Eagerly, the children ran forward to meet them.

'Ngaliba ngurlurringu' (We were afraid), said one of the men.' Barn-Barn Barlalalu yingathunu ngalibanha bawudu' (Barn-Barn Barlala has tricked us before). Barn-Barn Barlalau gamu ngalibanha biwarrjingalgu' (We must never let Barn-Barn Barlala trick us again).

BADUDU STORIES

These stories are dedicated to the caring staff
at Mount Margaret Mission whose names appear
in the stories, and also to the many others,
including my peers, whose names are not
mentioned.

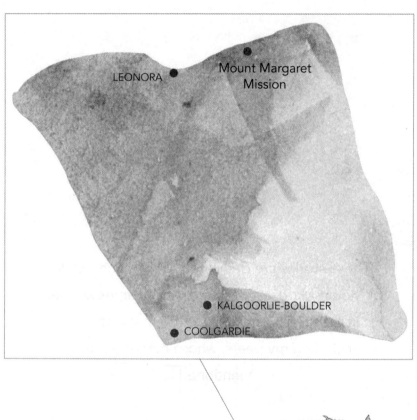

LEONORA

Mount Margaret
Mission

KALGOORLIE-BOULDER

COOLGARDIE

WONGUTHA COUNTRY
Eastern Goldfields, Western Australia

In the language of the Wongutha people, Badudu means 'not what it seems'. *Badudu Stories* is based on my clear memories of some of the difficulties we had in learning to speak English at Mount Margaret Mission. In many schools speaking 'native' was a punishable offence. At Mount Margaret it was different. Staff encouraged children to speak only English during school hours. They said it was the best way to learn a new language quickly and correctly. Outside school we were able to speak to each other in our own language.

As schooling was not compulsory for Aboriginal children, the Education Department had established no schools for us. The Missions chose to provide schools to give us the opportunity to learn as the non-Aboriginal children did. There were no qualified teachers at Mount Margaret but the Mission staff did what they could for us. It opened up a whole new world for me.

SMARTIE PANTS

'Good on you, Landy! Now you're good enough to play in the football team,' Mr Milnes nodded and smiled at him.

Landy felt excited. A wide grin spread slowly across his face. He couldn't wait to tell Tim.

Ever since they'd heard about the football match against Laverton School the boys had talked about it. They all wanted to play. They could think of nothing else. Every spare minute was spent kicking the football.

Landy was good at sport, but until he could speak English well enough to understand the rules of football he couldn't join the team. *Now*, his teacher had said he *was* good enough! He had been asked to play! He wanted to jump and shout and punch the air. He wanted to tell everyone.

Landy had often daydreamed about kicking goals from a tricky angle or taking the highest mark of the game.

Thana ngayunha nhagugu, (*Then everyone will notice me*) he'd think. Now at last he'd have a chance to make that dream come true.

The Mount Margaret boys practised every day. Landy would jump and mark the ball above the others' heads. He would try to trick his friends with sneaky handballs. They all wanted to kick goals.

Whenever Landy got a chance he would practise kicking drop-punts through the goalposts.

'Nhanganha garnbinha,' (This is a good game) he said to Tim one day.

But, there was one thing he couldn't do. As much as he tried, Landy could never snap the ball over his shoulder. Two of his mates were champions at it and Landy wanted to be like them. Whenever he could get a ball by himself he would practise that trick.

'You'll have to do better than that,' teased Tim when he caught Landy practising one day. Landy grinned. He knew his kick was getting much better.

At last the day of the football match arrived! As he jumped out of bed that morning Landy felt more excited than ever before.

He knew he had to be quiet in the dormitory, but he couldn't stop humming softly as he put on his clothes.

This is my first game, he thought again and again. *I'll never forget this day.*

The boys were too excited to eat. Breakfast seemed to take forever.

At last they were outside waiting for the truck. As soon as it arrived they all jumped on to get the best seats.

The thirty-two kilometre drive to Laverton seemed as if it would never end. Landy thought they'd never get there. It was over an hour later that the truck stopped at the Laverton School.

The boys pushed and shoved trying to get off

first and into the change room. Landy couldn't wait to put on his number six blue and gold guernsey.

The team looked good as they jogged on to the football ground. The oval was hard and dusty like the one at Mount Margaret.

'Barna nhanganha widu-widu. Ngaliba ngula murdi birrilgu,' (This ground is so hard. I bet we'll take lots of skin off our knees today) said Landy to his teammate. His mate nodded and kept jogging.

Landy wanted to play in the centre where he was free to move around, but the coach had told him to play at full-forward.

I don't care where I play, he thought. *I'm just glad I'm in the team.*

The players bunched together as the two captains met the umpire for the toss. The Mount Margaret team cheered as their captain pointed towards the end they would kick to first.

The boys jogged to their positions and the umpire took the ball. Everyone waited.

As Tim got to the sidelines he looked across

to his friend at full-forward. Although he was starting on the bench he was glad that Landy was on the ground now. He wanted him to kick a lot of goals. But more than anything else, he hoped that his friend would win the 'player of the match' award.

Tim watched Landy closely as he waited for the game to start. Was he feeling nervous too?

The ball was raised and the whistle blew. The umpire bounced the ball. The players were off. As the crowd yelled to their teams, Landy's whole body tingled with excitement.

The play went to the other end. Landy and his opponent jostled each other as they kept their eyes on the game.

I wish someone would kick the ball this way, Landy kept thinking.

Suddenly the ball *was* coming towards him.

Landy shot forward. His opponent tagged him closely. They jostled. Sideways, backwards, forwards, they bumped each other trying hard to get the front position. All the time Landy kept his eye on the ball.

With a burst of speed he left his opponent behind and took the mark on his chest.

The crowd went wild. 'Kick a goal, Landy! Kick a goal!' they yelled. The chant echoed around the ground. Everyone jumped up and down, shouting and waving. Then everyone was quiet. Landy was taking a shot for goal.

'Get lost, Landy! You're no good! You can't kick!' someone yelled.

That made Landy freeze. He'd never heard talk like this before. The children were taught to be good sports.

The umpire quickly beckoned Landy to his mark. Just as he was about to kick the ball, someone else yelled, 'Aren't you a smartie pants? You can't kick a goal from there!'

Landy stumbled, lost his concentration and kicked from the side of his boot.

The game went towards the other goals. He heard cheering and clapping at that end of the ground. Landy knew what that meant.

He punched his hand. He was mad with himself. He knew that he should've taken his time and not listened.

Mandi birni ngananha wathalgu? (I wonder what the boys will say?) he asked himself.

Then he frowned and looked down at his pants. *Smartie pants? Does that mean my pants are smart? I must ask Tim after the match.*

The game was fast and tiring. The lead changed often. Landy looked at the scoreboard. Mount Margaret sixty-eight points, Laverton sixty-eight points.

'Guthubanha marra,' (Kick another goal) he shouted to his team.

There were five minutes to go. Landy put everything into the game. He forgot all else. He just wanted to win.

The ball was kicked long into the forward line. It bounced in front of Landy and his opponent was about to tackle him. Without thinking, he snapped the ball over his shoulder. The roar was deafening. It was a goal!

The siren blared out. All eyes looked at the scoreboard for the final score.

'Ma nhawa! Ngaliba manu!' (Look! We've

won!) Landy grabbed a teammate by the arm. Although tired, both teams shook hands as they moved in to hear the 'player of the match' announcement.

'Landy of Mount Margaret,' boomed the loudspeaker.

The Mount Margaret people cheered and clapped as the players surrounded Landy.

As they walked to the change rooms Tim said to his friend, 'You were a bit slow to start, but then you played a great game.'

Landy puffed out his chest and smiled proudly. He was glad Tim didn't say anything about that bad kick.

On the way home in the truck, Landy whispered to his friend. 'I didn't know that pants could be smart.'

Tim sat thinking for a while. 'It doesn't sound right to me, but then I don't know everything.'

'Bundunggu mirrangu, "Dawithi nindi-nindiba!"' (Someone yelled, "Aren't you a smartie pants!") 'Dawithi nhanganha nindi-nindiya?' (Does that really mean my pants are smart?) Landy asked.

'Yeah, it could,' Tim replied. 'But let's check it out with Mr Milnes. He says we can ask him anything if we can't find it in the dictionary.'

On Monday, when school was over and the other children had all gone, Landy and Tim stayed behind.

'Nhurra ma thabila,' (You go and ask) Landy coaxed Tim. 'Nhurra tha gurnbi.' (You speak better English than me.)

Landy pushed Tim through the door. Tim walked straight up to his teacher. Landy followed.

'Excuse me, Mr Milnes,' said Tim, pretending to be brave. 'Can pants be smart?'

Mr Milnes turned and looked at the two boys. 'That depends,' he replied. 'Clothes can never be brainy or clever, only people can be that. But clothes can look smart.'

'The Laverton man yelled, "Aren't you a smartie pants!" What did he mean?' asked Tim.

'The man was trying to be funny. He was saying you're a know-all.'

'Oh, that's what it means,' said Tim. 'Thank you, Mr Milnes,' and the two boys walked off.

'Balu ngananha wathanhi?' (What did Mr Milnes mean?) Landy asked Tim.

'The man at the football said you're a know-all,' Tim grinned.

'Oh,' said Landy. 'What does that mean?'

'A show-off,' Tim explained.

'I'm not!' Landy didn't like that at all.

'Don't worry,' Tim nudged his friend. 'Some people will say anything to try to put you off. We know it's not true.'

'Do you think we'll ever really understand English?' Landy asked.

'Yes we will,' said Tim. 'Ngaliba wangga gutharratha.' (Then we will speak two languages.)

WHAT DO YOU SAY?

Buruwan was glad when Miss Jones said she was the most improved student in the class. She didn't know what it really meant, but by the look on her teacher's face, she guessed that meant something pretty good. But what did it *really* mean?

Buruwan had tried even harder since then.

'Please will you see me after school?' her teacher asked one day.

Buruwan looked up in surprise. That usually meant trouble. She glanced around at the others to see if they'd heard. They were bound to think that she'd done something wrong. They'd want to talk about it after school.

'I haven't been in trouble for a long time now,

so why do I have to stay in today?' she muttered to the boy next to her.

Buruwan wriggled to the edge of her chair so that she could snatch a glance at her friend. Laurel was already looking at her. When their eyes met, Laurel lifted the palm of her left hand and started to tap on it with two fingers of her right. Buruwan knew *that* meant trouble.

She took another quick glance at her teacher and shook her head. She was sure her friend was wrong. She could tell.

Miss Jonesnga wiya batha. Balu bugurlba. Ngayunha wiya warrgigu. (**Miss Jones isn't angry. She's happy. She won't growl at me.**) But the more Buruwan thought about it the more puzzled she became.

I think I know why I have to stay in, she told herself. *I'm getting a special award for being the most improved student, whatever that means. Miss Jones doesn't want the others to hear. But Jessie got an award last week and she didn't have to stay in …*

Buruwan let out a deep sigh and tried to

finish what she was doing. But she couldn't think straight.

Not long after, the bell rang and the children hurried out. The room became dead quiet. Buruwan felt nervous about staying in the classroom on her own. Her heart thumped and her stomach rolled and swirled as she tiptoed to the table and waited. She could hear her friends in the corridor whispering to each other. She guessed they'd have their ears pressed hard against the wall. They'd want to hear everything and be the first to pass it around to the others.

Miss Jones was busy at the blackboard. She wasn't in a hurry to speak to Buruwan.

'Ngalgarri, ngayu ngananha balhanu,' (Hurry up, I want to know what I've done) Buruwan said under her breath.

After what seemed like a long time, Miss Jones finished writing. She dusted the chalk off her hands and walked over to the cupboard.

Balu ngananha ngurriranhi? (*What's she looking for?*) Buruwan watched her closely.

'Now, where did I put it?' Miss Jones said,

as she hunted on the shelves. 'Aha, here it is.'
Turning around, she took a few steps towards
Buruwan.

*Guldungga ngananha? (What has she got
behind her back?)* Buruwan wondered.

Miss Jones looked straight into Buruwan's
eyes as she held out her hand to her. 'This is for
you. You've worked so well and I'm pleased with
you,' she said with a big smile. 'I hope you like
this. You'll have to work harder to get a few more
things to put into it.'

Buruwan's eyes bulged with excitement when
she saw the brand-new wooden pencil case. It
was just what she wanted. She wished she could
rush out now and yell it to everyone.

In Mount Margaret all the people shared
everything. The classroom was the only place
where the children owned anything.

*At last I've got something of my very own.
I really like it and I can keep it all to myself,*
Buruwan thought as she eagerly reached out for
it.

Instead of letting go, Miss Jones held onto the

pencil case. Buruwan looked up at her, surprised. *Why is she hanging on to my award? It's my pencil case. Balu ngayul dawarra yinganhi. (She's playing a game with me.)*

Well, I can get it off her, Buruwan thought.

She straightened. With one foot forward she lunged at the pencil case. Miss Jones didn't move. She just smiled and held on.

I'll try again. This time I'll use both hands. Buruwan pulled hard but nothing happened. *I can't win. Miss Jones is too strong.* She felt weak, but inside she was hopping mad.

'Haven't you forgotten something?' asked Miss Jones.

Buruwan turned around to look at her desk. Had she left something behind?

This is a dumb game. Miss Jones gives me a pencil case, then takes it back. Now she says I've forgotten something!

Buruwan felt angry and disappointed. What else could she do?

'What do you say, Buruwan?' Miss Jones asked.

There was a long silence. Buruwan stood with her head down and said nothing.

Why is Miss Jones asking a stupid question like that? Buruwan asked herself silently. *I don't want her silly old pencil case now. She can keep it.*

Miss Jones kept asking. 'What do you say, Buruwan?'

Buruwan kept silent.

'What a shame,' Miss Jones said at last. 'It's such a lovely prize and I would like you to have it. But if you won't say "thank you", you'd better go home without it.'

Buruwan was upset now. Tears popped up in her eyes as she thought about her pencil case. *How could anyone do such a mean and nasty thing?* She turned and half ran out of the room.

The others were waiting. When they saw her tears they all started to laugh and bellow at the top of their voices.

'Buruwan's in trouble and Buruwan is crying!' It didn't take long for others to join in. 'Buruwan's in trouble and Buruwan is crying.' The chant echoed loudly.

'Buruwan's in trouble and Buruwan is crying.'
Now everyone knew.

At last the children left her alone. Buruwan
ran to her secret hiding place. Covering her face
with her hands she cried and cried and cried. 'I
wanted that pencil case more than anything in
the world,' she gulped between her tears.

A big girl walking by heard the crying. She
stopped to see who it was. 'What's wrong with
you, Buruwan! Why are you crying?' she asked.

'Because I want to,' snapped back Buruwan.

'What's so special about crying? There must
be other things that you can do?'

'It's Miss Jones. She's the meanest person
in Mount Margaret. She won't let me have my
pencil case. She just holds on to it and won't let it
go.'

Violet listened. Bit by bit the whole story came
out.

'I'm never going to like her again,' cried
Buruwan.

'You will,' said Violet. 'But why won't you say
"thank you"?'

'We never do,' replied Buruwan, 'but Miss Jones makes a big fuss about it and punishes you if you don't. In the Wongutha way when someone gives you something, no one is expected to say "thank you". People give things because they want to.'

'I'll tell you something, Buruwan. I had to learn to say "thank you" too,' said Violet.

Buruwan stopped crying. She wiped her face with the back of her hand and looked up. 'Did all the older ones learn that too?' she asked.

'Yes, we all did,' answered Violet, 'and we still learn new things every day.'

Buruwan was quiet, then she asked, 'If I say "thank you" to Miss Jones, will she let me have my pencil case?'

'I would if it was me,' replied Violet. 'But why don't you ask her now?'

WHICH JACK?

When Wanu first came to live at Mount Margaret, he couldn't speak English. At home he spoke his own language and he knew lots of songs and stories as well.

School was hard because the lessons were in a language he couldn't understand.

'Ngayu munjong,' (I feel stupid) Wanu said to his friend one day. 'I wish I could speak like the other kids.'

'You will,' said Miyarn trying to help Wanu.

As he learned more words Wanu grew more sure of himself. Miyarn was a good friend. They were in the same class at school and they played together every day. Sometimes after school the two friends went exploring in the bush. At other times they played hop, step and jump. Talking together helped Wanu a lot.

'You hop like a kangaroo,' shouted Wanu as he tried to copy Miyarn.

'Hey, you speak English better than me!' Miyarn shouted back.

'Wiya,' (No I don't) said Wanu. 'Nyayu burdu gulainhi. Myayu tha munhthaba.' (It's hard to learn and I make a lot of mistakes.)

'You're not the only one,' agreed Miyarn, 'but we're getting better at it.'

Wanu was always glad when the school day was over, then he could talk in his own language. Wanu and Miyarn felt happiest when they could speak together in Wongi.

One day, after school, Miyarn and Wanu went to watch the men at the garage. They were working on the Red Terror, which was a big truck owned by the Mission.

'Ngananhthunu?' (What's wrong with it?) Wanu whispered to Miyarn.

'What's that?' Mr Jackson peered out from under the bonnet.

'What's wrong with it?' Wanu spoke more loudly, in English.

'Not much really,' said Mr Jackson. 'We're just giving it a good check over.'

The two boys crowded in and climbed onto a box beside the men. They peered under the truck's bonnet as the men worked. There were wires everywhere.

'What are these for?' asked Wanu.

'They join the different parts together and carry the power to make the engine go,' explained Mr Jackson.

'Oh,' said Wanu nodding.

'Nhurra nindirnda balu wathanhi?' (Do you know what he means?) whispered Miyarn. Wanu shook his head.

After a while, the other man turned to the boys and said, 'We're nearly finished here. We'll be working on the tyres next. What about getting the jack for us?'

Wanu and Miyarn nodded eagerly. They were pleased they could help the men. They scrambled off the box and hurried out of the garage.

Before long, the men finished working on the engine. 'Where's the jack?' Mr Jackson looked around. 'And where are the boys? I wonder where they've got to?' The boys were nowhere in sight and the jack was still in its place.

'I suppose they got bored,' said the other man, shaking his head. 'You know what kids are like.'

Sometime later, near knock-off time, Wanu and Miyarn came running back. Several of the boys followed.

'Where did you get to?' asked Mr Jackson. 'You were supposed to get the jack for us.' The two boys looked at each other in surprise.

'We have,' said Miyarn. 'First we couldn't find him, but then we did. Here he is!' Wanu pushed Jack forward.

He looked puzzled too.

The other boys started to giggle and laugh and point at Wanu and Miyarn.

Thana ngalibanha nhagul yigarringu. (They're laughing and poking fun at us.) Wanu couldn't work out why.

Ngaliba ngananha guyamada balhanu? (What did we do wrong?) he thought. *Ngaliba mandi nhanganha manu gnalhanu. (We got Jack for them.)*

The other boys kept on giggling and laughing. Wanu and Miyarn hung their heads and looked down at their feet. They felt shamed and upset.

'Hee-hee! Hee-hee!' laughed one of the boys. 'The men wanted the jack to hold up the truck, not Jack the boy! Hee-hee-hee!'

The other boys burst out laughing all over again. Wanu and Miyarn looked at each other without saying a word. Mr Jackson saw how upset they were. He felt sorry for them.

'Wait a minute,' he said to the others. 'Stop laughing! Remember *you* made mistakes when *you* learned English? We didn't laugh at *you*. We helped you and now you speak English well.'

The boys all nudged each other. The laughing stopped. Not a word was said.

Mr Jackson went on. 'Wanu and Miyarn will learn too if we help them, not tease them.' The other boys turned to look at each other and one by one, quietly left the garage.

Wanu stood close to his friend and asked, 'Thana dawarra wanga guyindanu ya?' (Did they get the words mixed up too?)

'Oh yes they did,' answered Mr Jackson.

The two friends walked off.

'This English is hard to learn,' Miyarn said.

'Yuwa mularrba,' (It sure is) agreed Wanu. 'It *sure* is!'

TOO BIG FOR YOUR BOOTS

'You're a busybody, Bindabinda,' Mr Walker
looked cross, 'and what's more, you're too big for
your boots!'

Grinning faces spun from every side of the
room to stare at Bindabinda. Their lips pushed
forward and pulled back again and again.
Bindabinda didn't need anyone to tell her what
that meant. This was Wongi sign language used
every day of the week. It was the people's way of
saying 'you poor thing'.

The boys quickly turned and looked at each
other, and then began nudging and whispering,
'Darda jimburn, darda jimburn.' (Pointy-toed shoes,
pointy-toed shoes.) They remembered. She had
been a big show-off in those second-hand shoes.

Bindabinda stopped. She slunk back to her desk. 'Nhurra ngurrju,' (You're selfish) hissed one of the boys. 'Nhurra dirdu guyamadangu.' (And you always spoil everything.)

Bindabinda turned to the boy. 'Tha libi,' (Big mouth) she snapped back at him. 'Balanha badudu.' (It's not what you think it means.)

'No, but he said you're too big for your boots! Ha, ha, ha,' the boy jeered.

Bindabinda was angry. She stuck out her tongue and answered back. '*You're* too big for your boots! Ha, ha, ha,' she mocked.

'Stop this nonsense at once and get on with your work!' Mr Walker's voice boomed.

'Nharru, balu nhurranh wathan wiirlthunu,' (You poor thing, you got told off) the whispers came back.

Bindabinda stretched out her bare feet and looked down at them. 'Stupid man. He can see I don't wear boots. I don't even wear shoes.'

The last time Bindabinda wore shoes was two years ago. That was when she first came to live at Mount Margaret Mission. She was too poor to have shoes of her own. The shoes she wore had belonged to her friend Skeet. They were a bit tight. They squashed her toes and gave her big blisters on the back of her heels. At first, Bindabinda had liked them. She thought she looked just 'it'. But then, when they began to hurt, she never wanted to wear them again.

Bindabinda twisted in her chair. She looked across at the feet of the girl in the next row, then back to her own. 'You're too big for your boots!' kept ringing in her ears. *Does this mean my feet are too small for my body?*

Bindabinda clearly remembered the Chinese story last week. It had told of binding little girls' feet so tightly that they hardly grew at all.

Bindabinda was worried. Did those pointy-toed shoes spoil her feet? *If I'm the only one with small feet it will be terrible. The kids would tease me all the time.* The more she thought about it, the more worried she felt.

On most days, the children treated each other like family, but if someone got into trouble, they'd never hear the end of it. 'Yarnangngu burlganha, jina thugurnhi,' (Big body, little feet) the children chanted whenever they saw Bindabinda.

Bindabinda hurried off to find Nari. She wanted to talk about it with her.

'What's wrong?' Nari called out as Bindabinda appeared from behind a tree. 'You look down in the dumps.'

'I am. The kids have all ganged up on me.' Bindabinda sounded as if she was about to cry. 'They follow me around and call me nasty names.'

'Whatever for?' Nari walked quickly towards her.

'It's all because of Mr Walker. He told everyone that I'm too big for my boots. Now the kids have taken it up.' Bindabinda tried hard to keep back her tears. 'I don't know what that means. I've looked in the dictionary, it doesn't say. I don't know where else to look. Do you know?'

'*I* don't have to look in the dictionary. *I* know all about it.' Nari always pretended to know everything. 'Your feet will stay tiny for the rest of your life, Bindabinda. You're going to look awful with small feet and a big body.'

'Don't talk like that, Nari!' cried Bindabinda. 'I don't want tiny feet. I want my *own* sized feet.'

Nari shook her head slowly. 'You'll *never* be the same as us. You'll be different.'

Bindabinda believed her. Nari was very good with words and she was always finding new ones to use. She spent a long time looking in the dictionary for them.

'I'll measure my feet every day. Then I'll know if you're telling the truth.'

'Ngayu wiya yarlamiyornhi. Ngayu nindi.' (I'm not lying. I know what it means.) Nari sounded quite sure.

'You're *never* going to wear grown-up shoes.'

Bindabinda was really worried now. No matter where she was, or what she did, she could never stop thinking about her feet. She felt sure everyone was talking about her. She sat under a peppercorn tree alone. Her head was full of whirling thoughts.

Ngayu mayi wiya ngalgu. Ngaba ngayugu yarnangu wiya burlgarrigu, (I'll stop eating. Then my body won't grow so big) she thought at last.

At every meal, she slowly pushed her food round and round in her mouth pretending to eat it. She swallowed very little.

As the days crawled by Bindabinda kept more and more to herself. She wanted to be alone to think about things.

'What's the matter with you, Bindabinda?' Mrs Jackson asked one morning. 'You don't look well. I'm taking you to the hospital to see Matron Murray.'

Bindabinda's heart jumped as she looked up. 'I'm all right, Mrs Jackson,' she answered quickly. 'I don't have to go to hospital 'cos I'm not sick.'

Bindabinda was scared of staying at the hospital. It was at the very end of the buildings and near lots of tall trees. Some of the children said the hospital was haunted. A hunchback ghost from way back in the past was often seen moving around. A scraping noise was always heard too. Thinking about it made Bindabinda's hair stand on end. She knew that she would be the only one in the hospital ward and she was quite sure the ghost would come.

Mrs Jackson took no notice of Bindabinda. She marched her over to the hospital and into the waiting room.

Bindabinda sat fidgeting while Matron Murray took her temperature. She made her poke out her tongue and say 'AAAH'. She pressed under her ears to see if she had the mumps. She checked her body for spots.

I wonder if Matron Murray will look at my feet? Bindabinda thought. *That's where the trouble is. I'll stick them out so she can see them.*

'I can't find anything wrong with you,' said Matron Murray at last, 'but I think I know what you really need. A good dose of castor oil.'

Bindabinda sat up and thought fast. *Yuk! I hate castor oil. I'll really be sick then. I'll have to tell her about my feet, so I won't have to take it.*

Matron Murray listened while Bindabinda told her story. She laughed softly, but made sure Bindabinda didn't hear. Matron Murray didn't want her to think she was laughing at her.

'Do you *really* think that your feet won't grow

anymore?' she asked quietly.

Bindabinda nodded. 'They must have stopped growing already.'

'Oh, no! "Too big for your boots" doesn't mean that at all. It means you think you know better than anyone else, and can do whatever you want to, instead of what you are told to do. When you learn more English, you'll understand better. Words can be very tricky.'

Matron's voice sounded kind. Bindabinda smiled slowly. She understood. 'So *that's* what it means. I'm not going to have small feet after all. I am glad about that!' She remembered what she was doing when her teacher had spoken those words.

'I was out of my seat and not taking any notice of Mr Walker when he said it.' She already felt better.

Bindabinda hurried off to put Nari right. *I wonder why Mr Walker twisted the words up so much? He should've said it straight out the first time.*

ABOUT THE AUTHOR

May L. O'Brien was born in the Eastern Goldfields of Western Australia in 1933. Her early life was steeped in Aboriginal culture, learning the many skills of hunting and gathering and listening 'to grannies and aunties that used to tell us stories around the campfire at night'.

At the age of five, May was taken to Mount Margaret Mission where she spent the next twelve years. May went on to train as a teacher and was the first known Aboriginal woman in Western Australia to graduate from a tertiary college.

May taught in Western Australian rural and metropolitan primary schools for twenty-five years, before becoming the first Superintendent of Aboriginal Education in Western Australia, a position she held until her retirement.

May was a passionate educator and a fearless activist who sat on many state and national committees. Among her many achievements, May won a Churchill Fellowship Award, was a delegate for Australia at the United Nations Conference of Women and was awarded a British Empire Medal and a John Curtin Medal for her work in education. She also was Patron of the Australian Principals Association Professional Development Council's 'Dare to Lead' project, the National Indigenous English Literacy and Numeracy Strategy Ambassador and an Ambassador for the Indigenous Literacy Foundation.

May L. O'Brien died in 2020.

PRONUNCIATION GUIDE

The following pronunciation guide was created by May L. O'Brien and is an approximation only. Some Wongutha sounds do not have an exact equivalent in English.

i	is pronounced as in it
ng	is pronounced as in sing
nh	is pronounced n as in thin
nn-yi	is a long n sound followed by a short y sound pronounced as in yip
rl	is a long r sound followed by a short l sound made with the tongue on the roof of the mouth
rn	is a long r sound followed by a short n sound made with the tongue on the roof of the mouth
rr	is a rolled r sound
u	is pronounced as in put

word	pronunciation	meaning
badudu	ba-du-du	not what it seems
balanha	bar-lar-nh-ar	that one / that thing

balhanu	balh-an-u	do / did / done / perform
balu	bar-lu	that person / he / she
barna	barn-a	ground
batha	ba-tha	angry / wild
Bindabinda	bin-da-bin-da	butterfly
birni	bi-rn-i	many
birrilgu	birr-il-gu	will scratch / graze
brinhba	bri-nh-bar	like / similar
bugurlba	bu-gurl-ba	happy
bundunggu	bun-dung-gu	a man has
burdu	bu-rd-u	can't / instead
burlganha	bu-url-gar-nh-ar	large / important one / boss
burlgarringu	burl-garr-ing-u	became larger / bigger
darda	dard-a	heel / high heels
dawarra	dar-warr-ar	with us / as well
garnbinha	garn-bi-nha	good / terrific / fantastic
guldungga	gul-dung-ga	behind back / on back
gutharra	gu-tharr-a	two
guthubanha	gu-thu-ba-nha	another one
guyamada	gu-ya-ma-da	wrong / no good
guyindanu	gu-yin-da-nu	do wrong / did wrong
jimburn	jim-burn	pointy
jina	ji-na	foot / feet
libi	li-bi	big
ma nhawa	ma nha-wa	look and see
marndi	marn-di	boy / uninitiated man
marra	ma-rra	get
ma thabila	ma tha-bil-a	go and ask
mayi	ma-yi	food
mirrangu	mirr-ang-u	yelled / shouted
mularrba	mu-larr-ba	it sure is / true
munhthaba	munh-tha-ba	making mistakes with words
munjong	mun-jong	idiot / dumb

murdi	murd-i	knee
ngalgarri	ngal-garr-i	hurry up
ngalgu	ngal-gu	eat
ngalhanu	ngalh-an-u	came / came by / came along
ngaliba	ng-ar-li-bar	us / we / us lot / all of us
ngalibagagu	ng-ar-li-bar-gar-gu	belonging to us / for us
ngananha	nga-na-nha	what is it? / what?
ngananhthuna	ngan-anh-thu-nu	what's wrong? / why is it so?
ngayu	nga-yu	I / me
ngayugu	nga-yu-gu	my / mine
ngayul dawarra	nga-yul da-warr-a	with me
ngayunha	nga-yu-nha	me
ngurrirranhi	ngu-rri-ra-nhi	looking for / searching for
nhagugu	nh-ar-gu-gu	see (have a good look)
nhagula	nha-gu-la	looking at
nhanganha	nhang-a-nha	this
nharru	nha-rru	you poor thing
nhurra	nh-u-rrar	you
nindi	nin-di	know
nindirnda	nin-dirn-da	know
tha	tha	mouth
tha garnbi	tha garn-bi	speak good English / speak well
thugunhi	thu-gu-nhi	little / small
wangga	wa-ng-gar	talk / speak
warrgigu	warr-gi-gu	growl at
wathan	wa-than	told
wathani	wa-tha-ni	saying
wiirlthunu	wiirl-thun-u	told off
wiya	wi-yar	never / will not / won't
yarlamiyornhi	yarl-a-mi-yornhi	telling lies / lying
yarnangu	yarn-ang-u	body
yigarrigornhi	yi-garr-i-gor-nhi	laughing
yinganhi	yin-ga-nhi	playing

Grandparents are special, and the time you spend with them is special, too. These charming tales share some exciting, happy and even scary times exploring country in bush and beyond.

BUSH AND BEYOND

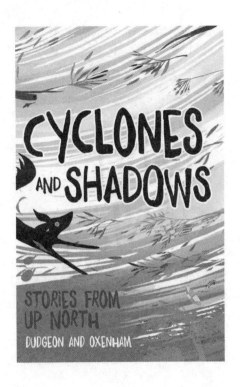

From an awesome sports car to a terrifying cyclone, from magical creatures to a haunted mango tree, these four stories from up north are full of adventure and excitement.

CYCLONES AND SHADOWS

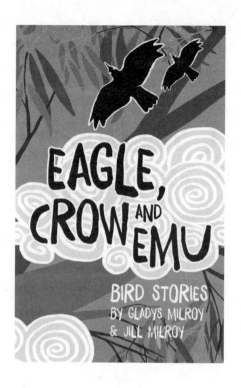

Birds who can't fly and snakes who can;
mistakes to be made and problems to be
solved; great enemies and even greater friends
— all this and more in three exciting stories full
of action, adventure and birds!

EAGLE, CROW AND EMU